THE CHILDREN'S CLASSICS Collection

Volume 2

Dados Internacionais de Catalogação na Publicação (CIP) de acordo com ISBD

A355l Alcott, Louisa May.
Little Women / Louisa May Alcott. - Jandira, SP : W. Books, 2025.
120 p. ; 12,80cm x 19,80cm - (Classics).

ISBN: 978-65-5294-116-9

1. Literatura americana. 2. Literatura estrangeira. 3. Clássicos. 4. Aventura.
5. História. I. Título. II. Série.

2025-2494 CDD 810
CDU 821.111-3

Elaborada por Lucio Feitosa - CRB-8/8803
Índice para catálogo sistemático:
1. Literatura americana 810
2. Literatura americana 821.111-3

Text based on the original story by Louisa May Alcott,
adapted by Lynne Wilson-Bailey
Illustrations by Roberta Bordone

1st edition in 2025
www.cirandacultural.com.br

Little Women

Louisa May Alcott

W. Books

Meg
Eldest sister

Jo
Second eldest sister

Beth
Second youngest sister

Amy
Youngest sister

Mrs March
Mother

Mr March
Father

Hannah
Maid

Aunt March
The sisters' aunt

Mr Laurence

Next-door neighbour of the March family

Laurie

Mr Laurence's grandson

Mr Brooke

Laurie's tutor

Professor Bhaer

Kind man who works in a boarding house

Mrs Chester

Friend of Aunt March

Chapter One

The four March sisters were quite close in age but very different in personality. As Christmas drew near, they sat discussing how unfair their life was. Their father had left to serve as a chaplain in the civil war and money was tight. Christmas would be bare.

'Christmas won't be Christmas without any presents,' grumbled Jo, the second eldest of the sisters.

chaplain
A Christian official who is responsible for religious services including wedding ceremonies and christenings.

She was fiery and independent, and insisted on being called Jo instead of her full name – Josephine.

'It's dreadful to be poor,' said Meg, looking down at her old dress. Meg was the eldest of the sisters. She loved

the luxuries they'd had before their father went away.

'I don't think it's fair that some girls have pretty things and others don't,' agreed Amy, the youngest of the sisters. She loved beautiful things and believed that girls were supposed to act gently and politely.

'We have Mother and Father and each other,' said Beth, the second youngest of the sisters, and the quietest. 'We can be grateful for that.'

'We do have a dollar each,' Jo reminded them, excitedly. 'Let's buy something for ourselves.

I'm desperate for a new book.' Jo loved reading, and writing stories was her greatest passion.

'I would like some new music,' whispered Beth. She loved to play the piano, but the one they had was old, worn and out of tune.

'I'd really like some new colouring pencils,' said Amy, the artist of the family.

'We've worked hard for that money, so we'll buy ourselves one item each for Christmas,' said Jo.

When their father left, the two eldest girls had found jobs to help out with the family income. Meg took a position as a governess, teaching young children. Jo went to work for their old, grumpy aunt, as a maid. She wasn't happy working for her aunt, but wanted to do her bit to help the family.

'I think I'm going to use my money to get Mother a new pair of slippers, instead of music for myself,' said Beth. She often put other people before herself.

governess

Someone who is responsible for the care and education of her employer's children.

Inspired by Beth's kindness, Meg, Jo and Amy also decided to buy gifts for their mother, instead of spending their money on themselves.

The girls awoke on Christmas morning. No stockings were hung over the fireplace and no presents sat under the tree. When they were dressed they traipsed downstairs. In the kitchen they found Hannah, their housemaid – but no Mother.

'Some poor boy came begging this morning and your mother went with him,' said Hannah as

she continued to get the breakfast things ready.

'Let's put Mother's presents in this basket for when she returns,' said Meg, taking a wicker basket out to display their gifts.

Shortly, Mrs March returned to the house. She looked lovingly at her daughters and the wonderful breakfast that Hannah had put together.

'I have something to ask of you girls,' she said. 'There is a poor family, the Hummels, not far from here. The dear mother has six children and a newborn baby. They have nothing. Would you be willing to give your breakfast to them, as a Christmas present?'

The girls stayed silent for a moment, looking at the breakfast laid out on the table before them. Their tummies rumbled. Then they snapped into action and gathered their favourite breakfast items.

'I knew you would do it,' said

Mrs March, smiling with pride at her generous girls. 'We'll all go round together.'

'Dinner is ready!' Hannah called to the family that afternoon. The girls followed the delightful smell coming from the dining room.

The dining table was laden with an incredible feast. Bowls of ice cream glinted under the light, a plump cake promised mouthfuls of delight and French bonbons were dotted in between other dishes. In the centre sat four bouquets of flowers. The sisters stared in amazement.

Mrs March smiled at her girls. 'It was our neighbour, Mr Laurence. He heard about the kind and generous thing you did for the Hummel family this morning and sent over these treats.'

'The old man who lives next door?' asked Beth. Mrs March nodded.

‘I wish I could send some of these beautiful flowers from Mr Laurence to Father,’ said Beth. ‘I fear he isn’t having a Christmas as nice as ours.’

Mrs March and her daughters joined together in one big hug. Although their father was not there to celebrate with them, they were happy that they had one another.

Chapter Two

One morning, Amy sat sketching while Beth was out helping the Hummels again. Jo was curled up in her favourite spot, writing an adventure story.

Meg burst into the room. 'Guess what!' she cried, beaming. 'Mrs Gardiner has sent me and Jo a New Year's Eve invitation for tomorrow night! Mother said we should go. What shall we wear?'

Jo knew that they only had a few dresses to choose from, as they didn't have much money. But she didn't care. She would much rather wear trousers than a dress, anyway.

'Oh, I wish I had a new dress made of silk,' sighed Meg. 'I'm afraid mine will look rather old and tatty compared to the elegant dresses the Gardiners will be wearing.'

'Your dress looks brand new,' said Jo. 'Mine is torn, with a burn mark on the back! It looks terrible.'

Meg was quite anxious at the thought of being seen as poor and unfashionable by the other guests. 'Well Jo, you must sit down all night so you don't embarrass us,' she said.

'I promise I'll be as prim and proper as I possibly can,' Jo sighed, folding her arms and turning away from her sister.

'Now, don't forget to keep that scorch mark out of sight,' whispered Meg as they approached the Gardiners' house the next evening.

prim and proper

'Correct' behaviour. Someone who is prim and proper is shocked by rude behaviour and words and would never act silly.

She touched her hair nervously. Mrs Gardiner gave them both a warm and kind welcome and left them with her own six daughters. Meg knew Sallie, the eldest of the Gardiner children, and she soon started to enjoy herself.

Jo, however, did not like girly gossip. She stood with her back to the wall to hide her marked dress, watching the dancing and wishing she could join in the fun.

She slid into a curtained area to sit down and keep her dress hidden. But there was already a boy there.

'Oh, I'm sorry!' said Jo. 'I didn't realise there was someone here. I'll go …'

'Don't worry. You can stay if you like,' replied the boy. 'I only came behind here because I don't really know anyone. I felt a bit out of place.'

Jo smiled. 'Me too.' Then she held out her hand. 'I'm Jo.'

'I'm Laurie – Laurie Laurence.' Jo soon realised he must be Mr Laurence's grandson. He lived next door to them!

'Why aren't you dancing with the others?' Laurie asked. 'Don't you like to dance?'

'I do if there is plenty of room,' said Jo. 'I'm likely to step on people's toes and knock something over in a place like this. I'm best keeping out of the way. Then I won't embarrass my sister, Meg.'

Laurie thought for a moment and then a mischievous grin spread across his face.

'Come with me,' he said. Jo followed him into the large hallway. There was no one there and plenty of room. Laurie took

Jo's hand and taught her a German dance. When the music stopped, they collapsed on the stairs to catch their breath, laughing.

Then Meg appeared in the hallway, limping. She had hurt her ankle while dancing.

‘It hurts!’ she cried. ‘I want to go home, but how will I walk?’

‘I can drop you both home in my carriage,’ offered Laurie. Jo thought about just how wealthy the Laurences must be to own a private carriage.

‘It’s still early,’ said Jo. ‘Do you not want to stay longer?’

‘Oh, I always leave parties early,’ said Laurie, looking down at his feet. ‘I don’t know anyone here. It won’t be as much fun when you have gone.’

Jo was as delighted as Laurie to have made a new friend.

Chapter Three

A few weeks later, Jo stopped by at the Laurences' house to keep Laurie company as he'd been unwell. The Laurences' house was a large property with huge, well-kept gardens. It was luxurious with a big coach house and conservatory, and thick curtains hanging in the windows. The March house was much smaller.

'This is a grand old house! How many people live here?' asked Jo.

'Just Grandpa and me,' said Laurie.

'It must get lonely.'

'It does, but I have my books for company,' Laurie replied.

'Books?' said Jo, perking up. 'What kind of books?'

Laurie grinned. 'Come downstairs and see.'

When they got to the library, Jo squealed in delight. The room was lined with books from floor to ceiling. Statues were placed around the room and there was a large open fireplace to sit comfortably by.

'What richness!' Jo exclaimed. 'Laurie, you must be the happiest boy alive with all of these books.'

'A boy can't live on books alone,' said Laurie, with a shy smile. Jo smiled back. Laurie didn't have siblings to keep him company, as she did. But she thought that she could become like a sister to him.

Suddenly, a voice came from the back of the room, making Jo jump. 'What have you been doing with that boy of mine?'

Jo turned to see Mr Laurence stroll into the library. 'Just being neighbourly, sir, and trying to

cheer him up.'
The old man studied Jo, who stood with a large book in her hands. He smiled.

'Come and join us for tea,' said Mr Laurence.

A strong friendship quickly bloomed between the two households. Laurie was as welcome in the March house as the sisters were welcome in his. Mr Laurence especially loved having Beth visit, as she played his old piano, filling the house with music again. Laurie enjoyed the company of all four sisters. However, Jo had quickly become his best friend.

One evening, Laurie invited Jo and Meg to the theatre. Amy was cross. She wanted to go, too, but she wasn't allowed. She had been in bed all week with a terrible cold.

'No,' said Jo in a firm manner. 'Mother has told you to stay home. She said she will take you next week.'

'But I'm feeling much better,' Amy pleaded. 'I won't be a

nuisance. You won't even know I'm there.' Amy hated being told no, especially by Jo, who was always bossing her about.

'We could take her and bundle her up,' said Meg, stroking Amy's face. 'I'm sure Mother wouldn't mind.'

'No,' said Jo again. 'Laurie has only got three tickets. You can't come this time, Amy, and that's that.'

'I'll make you pay for this, Jo!' Amy sobbed, as her sisters left the room. Upset that she had been left out, Amy had an idea. The one thing

Jo prized more than anything was her precious writing book. Jo was always writing stories and poems. Amy found the book, took it to the fire and threw it in.

'That will show her,' Amy sulked, watching Jo's book burn in the flames. 'Now she'll know how it feels to be this upset.'

Chapter Four

The next day, Meg, Beth and Amy were sat together in the living room when Jo walked into the room in a panic.

'Has anyone seen my book?' she asked her sisters. 'I want to add more stories to send to Father.'

Meg and Beth both shook their heads. Amy stayed quiet and poked the fire.

Jo noticed Amy's quietness. Her sister's face had gone red, too.

'You have it!' she said to Amy.

'No, I haven't,' said Amy.

'You're lying!' shouted Jo, grabbing Amy by the shoulders.

'You'll never see your silly little book again,' Amy grinned. 'I burnt it.'

Jo turned very pale. 'You burnt my book? You wicked little girl!' She shook Amy in a rage.

Meg rushed over to rescue Amy. Beth tried to calm Jo's temper, but it was no use. Jo smacked Amy around the head before running out of the room, crying.

When Mrs March heard the

story later, she spoke to Amy and made her see how hurtful her actions were. Even Beth, who saw the best in everyone, was disappointed in her younger sister.

When Amy realised the impact of her actions, she felt terrible and extremely guilty. That evening, she begged Jo for forgiveness. But Jo said, 'I shall never forgive you.'

It had been a week and Jo was still finding it extremely difficult to shake off her anger with Amy.

She thought that a skate on the frozen river with Laurie would calm her down.

After Jo had left to get her skates, Amy asked Meg, 'Do you think Jo will ever forgive me?'

'You were awful to her. Wait until Jo is feeling happier, and then she just might be in the right mood to forgive you,' replied Meg. Amy didn't waste a second. She grabbed her skates, and followed Jo and Laurie to the river.

Jo heard Amy calling her name behind her, but she didn't stop and wait. As soon as she got to the river she put her skates on and flew onto the ice with Laurie, leaving Amy behind.

'Stay at the side where the ice is thickest! The middle isn't safe,' Laurie called. Jo heard him but Amy didn't.

Suddenly, Amy screamed. Jo spun around just in time to see her sister fall through the ice in the middle of the freezing river. Jo tried to move towards her, but terror held her in her place. As Jo's heartbeat drummed in her ears, Laurie rushed past her. With an almighty effort they managed to pull Amy out of the icy water.

Jo and Laurie got Amy back home, shivering and dripping. They wrapped her in blankets and laid her in front of the fire.

Later, as Amy slept, Jo cried to her mother. 'If Amy dies I'll never forgive myself.

I was so angry with her that I left her behind on the ice. If anything happens to her it will be my fault.'

'She's quite safe,' her mother assured her. 'You and Laurie did the right thing bringing her back here and getting her warm. She will be fine.'

But Jo couldn't help but be angry with herself. 'It's my awful temper. One minute I think I have it under control, and the next it bursts out of me more than ever. What can I do about it?'

Mrs March smiled. 'We can work to improve ourselves, every day.

My temper is just as bad as yours, if not worse. It's taken me years to learn how to control it,' she said. 'Never stop trying to better yourself, Jo.'

All of the anger Jo had felt towards Amy had disappeared. Jo had forgiven Amy's act, and she now needed to forgive herself.

Chapter Five

As the weeks passed by, Jo and Amy grew closer again. As the creative members of the family, they spent time together, with Jo encouraging Amy's drawing and Amy reading Jo's new writing.

Meg was leaving the family house for a few days of fun with some friends. They were to attend the house of a wealthy family who put on fancy parties. Meg only had one ball dress. It was old and worn but she was proud of it – until she was getting ready with her friends. They turned their noses up at it and left her feeling insecure.

When the girls insisted on dressing Meg up in their old clothes, she agreed. Even her friends' old clothes were much more fashionable and expensive than Meg's 'best' dress. They did her hair, her make-up and clothed her in fine jewellery and feathers.

The eldest March sister felt very grand as she headed down to the party.

That evening, she danced with all of the other guests. She felt so happy she could burst. But when she stopped for a rest, she overheard a conversation that hurt and embarrassed her.

'That March sister looks like a silly doll dressed up in that dress. She usually looks so lovely,' said one guest to another. Meg looked down at her fancy dress and ran off, crying.

When Meg returned home, Mrs March asked her how her trip was.

‘I’ve been a fool, Mother. I was so ashamed about us not having much money that I forgot who I was for a while. I pretended to be someone I’m not. I just wanted to be happy and accepted in the rich and fashionable world. But then I heard someone say something awful about me.’

‘Happiness doesn’t come from money,’ said Mrs March. ‘I’d rather see my girls happy and married to poor men, than unhappy and married to rich men.’

When summer came, Laurie had some visitors all the way from England. Laurie wrote Jo a note inviting her and her sisters to join them for the day. There would be games, a picnic and rowing on the river.

The group of visitors were the Vaughn family: Kate, who was the eldest; Fred and Frank, the twins; and Grace, the youngest. Laurie's tutor, Mr Brooke, also came along for the fun.

The party set off in a couple of row boats and floated along the river. Meg was pleased to find herself in the same boat as Mr Brooke, whom she secretly liked. He wasn't a rich man but he was kind and had lovely manners. Meg felt comfortable with him.

After rowing, the morning was spent playing croquet and laughing in the sun. When it was time for lunch, Mr Brooke asked Meg to help him lay the table. As they ate, everyone noticed how Mr Brooke couldn't take his eyes off Meg.

Jo, Beth and Amy whispered to each other, grinning at the budding romance.

When it was time to end their afternoon, the March sisters were escorted home.

'American girls are very nice when one gets to know them,' said Fred to Mr Brooke, when the afternoon was over.

'I quite agree with you,' said Mr Brooke as he fondly thought of Meg.

Summer quickly turned into autumn. Meg, Jo and Mrs March

were looking out at the frostbitten ground when Hannah burst into the room with a telegram in her hand. Mrs March read it at once. Her hands trembled and she dropped into a chair.

URGENT DELIVERY WITHOUT DELAY

TELEGRAM

Mrs March
Your husband is very ill.
Come quickly.

S. HALE
Blank Hospital, Washington.

telegram

A telegram is a short message that is sent by electric signals between two electrical stations and then printed out onto paper. A telegraph is the system used to send telegrams.

Mrs March turned to her daughters. 'I shall go at once, but it may be too late. Oh, children!'

They quickly arranged for Mrs March to leave on the next train. The sisters couldn't help but weep, and tried to console one another with tender words.

Mr Laurence was informed of Mrs March's plans and insisted on watching over the sisters. Mr Brooke offered to accompany Mrs March to Washington.

Mrs March was gone for weeks, but she wrote to the girls often.

One evening Meg read a letter aloud to her sisters.

Dear girls,

Your father is doing much better, although he is still not well enough to travel. Mr Brooke has been ever so kind. He is helping me nurse your father. I don't know what I'd do without him here.

I promise we'll be back as soon as we can. Look after each other and don't forget to check in on the Hummels. They will need your help, especially in the colder weather.

Much love,

Mother

The girls rejoiced to hear that their father was improving, and Meg was especially happy to hear that Mr Brooke had been helpful.

'I'm so pleased Mr Brooke went with mother,' she told her sisters. 'What a kind and thoughtful man he is.'

Chapter Six

'I wish you would go and check on the Hummels,' Beth said to her sisters. Beth had taken their mother's departure the hardest. She often hid herself away in a cupboard to cry, so her sisters wouldn't see and be made sadder. But she had also followed their mother's wishes to look after their poor neighbours.

'I'm too tired today,' replied Meg. 'Jo, you should go.'

'Sorry, I want to finish working on my novel,' said Jo.

'Why don't you go yourself?' Meg asked Beth.

'I've been every day,' replied Beth. 'The children are sick and I don't know what to do for them.'

'Amy will be home soon. She can go,' said Meg.

After an hour of waiting, Beth got ready to go herself, filling a basket with things for the Hummel children. Her sisters didn't notice her leave. It was late when she returned, and they didn't hear her come back either.

Later that evening, Jo found Beth in the medicine cupboard.

'What are you doing?' she asked her younger sister.

'The doctor said the Hummel children have scarlet fever. I haven't had scarlet fever before, and the doctor said I need to take medicine so I don't catch it. You and Meg have both already had it, so you'll be OK.'

'Oh, Beth! If you get sick I'll never forgive myself. You've been there every day!' wailed Jo. 'If only Mother were home.'

scarlet fever

An illness with flu-like symptoms that can make you feel very poorly.

'Send Amy away to Aunt March's for the time being. If I've caught it, we don't want her to get it, too,' said Beth, looking tired.

Amy was not happy at being carted off to their notoriously grumpy old aunt, but her sisters insisted.

The doctor came to the Marches' house and confirmed their fears. 'I'm afraid that Beth has scarlet fever. She must be put to bed at once. She needs plenty of rest and plenty of water. I will come and check on her in a few days.'

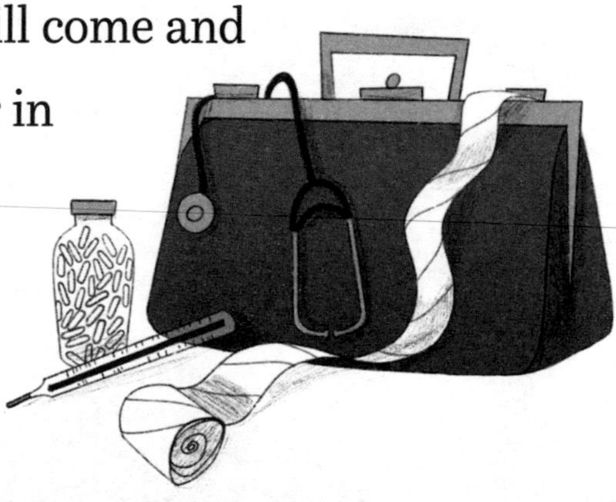

'Thank you, Doctor. I will nurse her back to health,' said Jo.

'I'm the oldest, Jo. I should be the one to nurse her,' Meg replied.

'No, Meg. I let her go out in the cold every day. I put my writing first, when I should have helped her. I'll look after her.'

As the days passed, Beth's illness grew worse. Jo sat by Beth's bed every day, even though she spent most of the time sleeping.

'Your sister is very ill,' said the doctor. 'You must think about sending for your mother.'

Jo left Beth's bedside and sought comfort from her best friend next door.

'Is it really that bad?' asked Laurie.

Jo nodded as the tears streamed down her face. 'I'm sending a telegram to Mother. She needs to come home.'

Laurie rubbed Jo's back tenderly. 'I sent a telegram yesterday and Mr Brooke answered it. She's already on her way.'

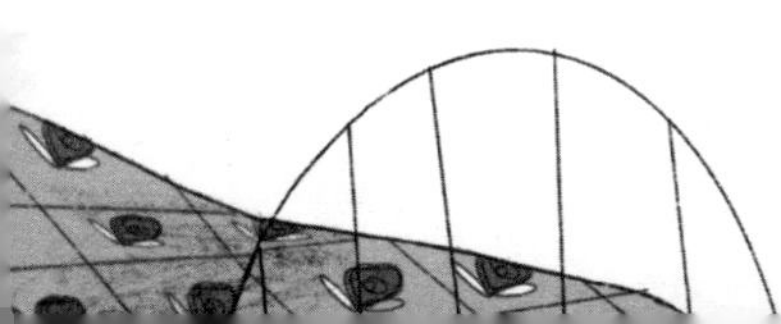

Jo looked up and hugged him. ‘Oh Laurie, thank you!’ She cried some more and kissed his cheek.

Laurie smiled bashfully. He had once thought of Jo as a sister. But lately he was beginning to feel something more.

Jo sat with Beth all night, convinced they were going to lose her. Jo was exhausted, but she wouldn't let herself lie down in case she fell asleep and Beth's temperature grew worse. She fought to stay awake and care for her younger sister. Jo cooled Beth's forehead with a damp towel, helped her sister take sips of water and held her hand all night. By the morning there was a different look on Beth's face. She didn't look as though she was in pain and there was a slight colour to her cheeks.

Mrs March returned home that night with a warm embrace for her girls. She sat with Jo, watching over

Beth as she slept, never leaving her sick daughter's side. It appeared that Beth was finally on the mend.

'Mr Brooke stayed in Washington to look after your father, while I came home,' said Mrs March. 'There are many hard times in life, but we can always bear them if we accept help from friends.'

'I want to tell you something, Mother,' said Jo. 'Laurie told me the other evening that Mr Brooke cares deeply for Meg.'

'You don't seem happy about this, Jo,' said Mrs March.

Jo sighed. 'I'm not sure I'm ready

for Meg to get married and leave us. I wish we could just stay together.'

Mrs March smiled and put her arm around Jo.

'I do believe that Mr Brooke loves Meg. He told me so while we were away. But Meg is only seventeen and too young for marriage. I have told him that if she loves him when she is twenty, he can ask her to marry him. He is a good man and very generous. He is not rich in money, but rich in kindness. Don't worry, dearest Jo. Your sister will not leave for a while yet.'

Another Christmas soon came around. Although the girls were missing their father, the family were joined by Mr Laurence and Laurie, and spirits were high.

Beth was still weak from her illness but overjoyed at the festivities. 'I'm so full of happiness! The only thing that could make this more perfect would be Father being home,' she said.

Then, there was a knock at the door. Laurie went to answer it. He returned shortly with

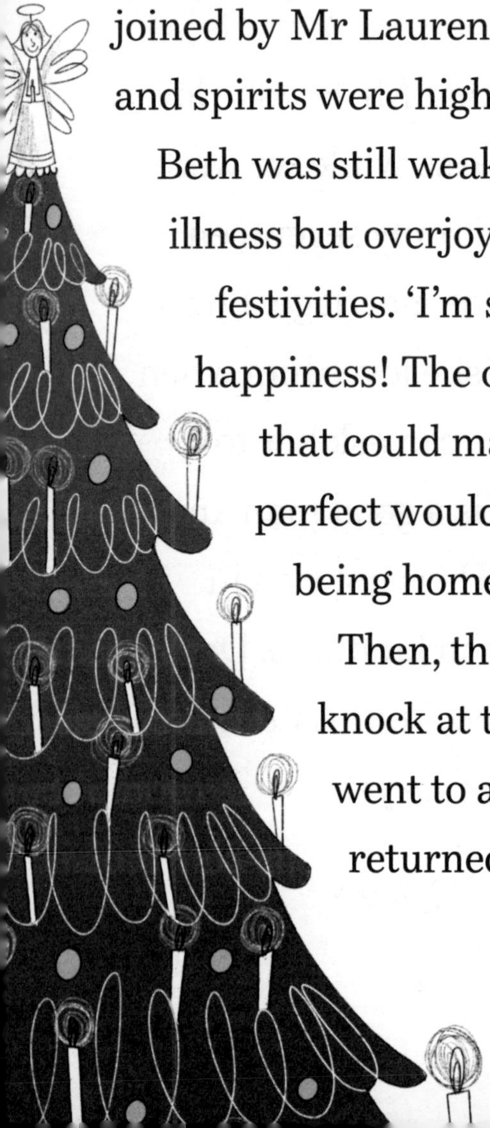

an excited look on his face. 'One more Christmas present for the March family,' he said. He moved away from the door to reveal a tall figure behind him.

The girls squealed in delight and ran forwards to their father. Mr March became invisible in the embrace of four pairs of loving arms. The family were finally together again.

Never had there been a happier Christmas dinner than there was that day. The family revelled in a plump turkey, plum pudding and delicious jellies, while they caught Mr March up on everything that had happened while he had been away. It was a great reunion and the best Christmas Day the family had ever had.

Chapter Seven

Three years after the return of Mr March, Mr Brooke asked Meg to marry him. John Brooke wasn't a rich man and they couldn't afford a fancy lifestyle. But he was patient and loving, and their future seemed bright.

'John is good and wise and works hard. I'm so happy to know that he loves me,' Meg said to Mrs March one afternoon, while they were preparing for the wedding.

‘He has done a lot for our family,’ agreed Mrs March, smiling at her daughter.

Meg and Mr Brooke married in June. They had a beautiful outdoor wedding, with their closest friends and family present.

They moved into their own little cottage, and it wasn’t long before two new additions joined the family. Meg had twins: a boy called Demi and a girl called Daisy. Her little family was complete and kept her very busy. She may not have been rich, but her happy family was all she needed.

With Meg no longer living in the March house, Jo felt a little lost. She was being paid a dollar a column for writing short stories in a newspaper. Jo's dream was to write great novels. The columns were not like the adventure stories she was passionate about writing, but she was proud to be earning an income to help her family.

Determined to achieve her true ambition of becoming an author, Jo filled every spare minute reading and writing her novel.

One afternoon, she came across an advert in the newspaper.

> **$100 PRIZE!**
>
> **For the best short story. Entries to be in by July 2nd. Winner will be notified by post in September.**

This was it! Even if she didn't win, this was Jo's chance to get a professional publisher to read her work. Jo decided not to tell her family about entering, in case she didn't win. She worked energetically on her piece and sent it off.

It was a long nine-week wait. As September came, Jo anxiously awaited the post each day. Finally, she received a letter.

'Mother! Father! I won!' cried Jo, running into the living room.

'Won what, dear?' asked Mrs March. Jo then told the family about her competition entry.

'What will you spend the money on?' asked Amy excitedly, thinking about all the lovely things they could buy.

Jo imagined, for a moment, spending the money on books, notebooks and theatre tickets.

But she shook those thoughts from her mind. She knew how she wanted to spend the money. Beth had never fully recovered from the scarlet fever. She was a happy and hopeful seventeen-year-old, but not as healthy as she once had been.

Jo turned to her mother. 'I'd like to pay for you and Beth to go to the seaside. The sea air will help Beth's health. It will do her so much good.' Mrs March couldn't speak. Her eyes welled up with tears and she burst with pride for Jo.

Following her competition success, Jo kept working on her novel. After she'd been to see the local publisher one afternoon, Jo gathered her family at home. She was feeling a little confused and wanted her family's advice.

Beth was the first to notice Jo's strange mood. 'What's the matter?' she asked.

‘The local publisher has agreed to publish my first novel. He’s going to pay me 300 dollars for it,’ Jo replied.

‘Oh Jo, that’s wonderful!’ exclaimed Beth. ‘But, what’s wrong?’

Jo sighed. ‘They want me to delete a third of the story.’

‘If you want it published, you should do what the editor says. They know what sells, after all,’ said Amy.

‘Why the rush to publish it?’ asked Mr March. ‘If you don’t want to delete part of the story, why don't you spend more time working on it and then try again?'

'As family, perhaps we are too close to be the best judges,' Mrs March reflected. 'Maybe it will be best to get it out into the world. Whatever praise or criticism you get should be useful for future novels.'

The conflicting advice confused Jo. Eventually she decided to do as the publisher asked. She cut down the manuscript and returned it to them for publication.

When it was printed, Jo received the money – but also very

mixed reviews. Some thought it was a fine first novel. Others thought that it seemed incomplete. Jo read these reviews with frustration.

‘I wish I had argued my point and published the whole novel. And these reviews don’t tell me anything useful!’ Jo complained. ‘I don’t know which criticism to take as advice and which to ignore.’

The family gave her words of comfort and encouragement. Jo decided to take note of the criticism from those who were the most experienced in writing, and to learn from it whenever she decided to write her next book.

Chapter Eight

As the years had passed, Amy had taken on Jo's former work looking after their old Aunt March. Aunt March rewarded Amy by paying for her to have art classes. Amy loved that she could spend her time painting and drawing, and also earn money to help her family.

Jo had worked hard to control her temper since the incident when Amy had fallen through the ice. However, she still hated being expected to behave politely and daintily at social events. So when Amy asked Jo to accompany her to a social tea party with their neighbours and aunt, she wasn't happy.

'I'll do anything for you, Jo, if you'll only dress nicely and behave well,' Amy bargained.

'If people care more about my clothes than they do about me, I don't wish to see them!' Jo replied.

‘You can dress nicely for us both and be as elegant as you please.’

‘Jo, be a friend and help your little sister. Please don’t embarrass me,’ said Amy.

‘I promise I’ll be calm, cool and quiet. I can just about manage that,’ huffed Jo.

Jo couldn’t help but be sullen at the tea party. For every question she answered with a simple ‘yes’ or ‘no’. Amy sent her warning glances, urging her moody sister to talk to the hosts.

‘How are you with languages?’ one neighbour, Mrs Chester, asked Jo.

'I hate them,' replied Jo. 'I can't bear French. It's a silly language.'

As Jo and Amy left the house, they heard a very clear remark from one of the ladies. 'What a rude, uninteresting girl that Jo March is!'

A week later Mrs March received a letter and went to join Jo and Beth in the living room. Seeing their mother's excitement, the girls demanded to hear the news.

'I've had a letter from Mrs Chester. She's going abroad to Europe next month and wants Amy to go with her.'

'What? That's not fair! I've always wanted to go abroad,' said Jo.

'Well, it's partly your own fault,' said her mother calmly. 'Mrs Chester says you were rather rude at the tea party. She said your manners are too blunt.'

'It is selfish of me, but I'm glad

I will not be losing you,' said the sickly Beth, hugging her older sister.

Jo was furious at herself for her attitude at the Chesters' tea party, and upset that it stopped her being able to travel. But she managed to cool down and join in with the celebrations by the time Amy came home from their aunt's and learnt the news.

'Now I can pursue my painting abroad!' said Amy. 'If I have any artistic genius at all, I will find out in Rome.'

Jo was happy that Amy would

be able to follow her passion. But she was sad, too, that her sisters were beginning to separate from the home they had grown up in together.

Soon the time came for Amy to depart to Europe. She hugged her parents and sisters goodbye, tears flowing down her cheeks. Laurie had come out to say goodbye too. Amy hugged him last and pleaded, 'Please take care of them for me.'

Laurie promised that he would.

Chapter Nine

Amy wrote home from every stop on her trip.

Dear Mother, Father and sisters,

I'm having a lovely time! London is a wonderful place. Guess who I met up with? Laurie's English friends, Fred and Frank Vaughn. It's been great spending time with them. Fred seems to be very fond of me. They've showed us a jolly good time, taking us to theatres, parties, parks and all the usual tourist sites.

Love,

Amy

Dear Mother, Father and sisters,

Paris is as fabulous as I had hoped. I've had a lovely surprise as Fred has showed up in Paris, too.

We're off to Germany and Switzerland next!

Love to you all,

Amy

Amy was off having adventures abroad, Meg was busy with family life now she was married – and now Laurie was off to college as well. This left Jo at home with Beth, feeling left behind.

Whenever Laurie came home to visit, Jo noticed he seemed intent on being her boyfriend and not just a friend. Jo felt uncomfortable with the change. She wanted to stay as Laurie's best friend, not his girlfriend.

Jo approached her mother one evening. 'I want to go away somewhere this winter, for a change.'

'Where will you go?' asked Mrs March.

'I was thinking I could go to New York, to help in a boarding house. I could teach the children to sew.'

'Go to work in a boarding house?' Mrs March said, surprised. 'But what about your writing?'

'I need life experience to make my writing more interesting. How can I write about new places and situations if I don't go anywhere or do anything?' said Jo.

Mrs March knew her daughter well, and she sensed there was something Jo wasn't telling her. 'Is this your only reason for wanting to go?'

> **boarding house**
> A house where people rent a room to sleep in and share a kitchen, food and social space with others. The lodgers could be men, women, and families.

‘No, Mother,’ Jo admitted. ‘I’m afraid Laurie is getting too fond of me. I need to get away to give him time to stop feeling this way.’

‘You don’t feel that way about Laurie?’

‘I love him as a friend, but that’s all,’ said Jo with a sigh.

Jo soon moved away from home to broaden her horizons, as she had hoped. She travelled to New York, where she began her work as a governess at a boarding house. She also wrote popular fiction for a magazine in the city. She did not like the stories she was writing and worried about her progress as a serious author. But the magazine did earn her money to send back to her struggling family. She decided that was more important than her satisfaction.

Jo wrote home often, missing her parents and Beth, but it didn't take her long to settle in to her new surroundings. She quickly became friends with a German man who was lodging at the boarding house and teaching the children German.

'You're so lovely with the children, Professor Bhaer,' she said to him one afternoon. She had just witnessed the professor read to the children outside of his lesson time.

'I love teaching the children and reading to them, plus I like to help out where I can,' Professor Bhaer replied. 'Now tell me, do you read German?'

'No, I've never learnt,' said Jo.

'If you would like to learn, I shall

teach you,' he said with a smile.
Jo was touched by his kind gesture. Even though she didn't enjoy learning languages, she found that she was looking forward to spending more time with Professor Bhaer.

One afternoon, Jo stumbled against a door in the corridor, and it flew open. Inside, the professor was sat in his dressing gown sewing a sock.

Jo was embarrassed. 'I'm so sorry! I didn't mean for the door to open.'

'It's no bother,' he replied, laughing.

The sight of him sewing gave Jo an idea. 'I know,' she said, 'why don't I do your sewing as a thank you for you teaching me German?'

'It's a deal,' he agreed with a smile.

Jo thought how handsome he looked.

As they spent more time together, Jo grew fond of Professor Bhaer. She often found him playing with the children, allowing the young ones to clamber over him. It was clear how his clothes became torn and shabby, and she admired his kindness.

Professor Bhaer took the time to read Jo's magazine stories, but Jo was embarrassed. They did not represent her best work.

'You should follow your heart and write the stories you really want to,' said the professor encouragingly.

‘I love how much we have in common,’ said Jo. ‘We both enjoy writing, we both love books, and we both love learning new things. I’ll be sad when the time comes for me to leave.’

‘I will be sad too,’ agreed the professor.

Finally, the time did come for Jo to leave. As she left, she promised Professor Bhaer that they would meet again.

I’ve made a friend worth having and I’ll try to keep him my whole life, she thought as she waved goodbye to Bhaer and to New York.

Chapter Ten

Jo returned home in time for Laurie's college graduation. She was delighted to be reunited with her friend.

'You'll come and see me tomorrow?' he asked Jo.

'I'll come, rain or shine!' she laughed. Laurie looked at her affectionately, and suddenly Jo felt worried that he might still love her as more than a friend.

After a moment, Laurie took

her hand. Jo felt fear in the pit of her stomach. 'I've loved you since I met you, Jo. And my feelings are only growing,' he said.

'Laurie, don't say that,' pleaded Jo. 'I'm fond of you and very proud of you. But I don't love you in that way.'

Laurie looked crushed. 'Don't tell me that Jo, I can't bear it.'

Then he said, 'Do you love that German man? The professor back in New York that you were always writing about?'

'Professor Bhaer has nothing to do with this, Laurie. You think of me as a girlfriend, but I don't think of you as a boyfriend,' she said. 'You'll find someone else to love and you'll forget about all this.'

'I'll never love anyone more than I love you,' cried Laurie, before storming off. Jo's heart ached as she realised that this may be the end of their friendship.

'I'm sorry she doesn't love you in the same way,' said Mr Laurence when Laurie told him Jo had broken his heart. 'Come with me to Europe for the summer. The change will do you good.'

So Laurie went to Europe in a bid to forget his love for Jo.

More letters from Amy had arrived while Jo was away in New York.

Jo sat down to read through them and find out how her sister was getting on in Europe.

Dear Mother, Father and sisters,

I'm in Germany now! Fred has come with us. He took me on a moonlit boat ride on the River Rhine – it was the most romantic trip.

I don't know if I am in love with Fred, but he is generous and wealthy. His money could really help our family. If he asks me to marry him, I'm going to say yes.

I'll write again soon.

Love,

Amy

Dear Mother, Father and sisters,

Switzerland is beautiful. I'll get straight to the point, as I'm sure you're dying to know. Fred hasn't asked me to marry him yet. We recently had some horrible news. His brother Frank is ill, and Fred had to leave immediately.

Fred said he'd come back for me and to not forget him. But, for now, we are travelling alone again. I am looking forward to getting to Rome, where I can focus on my art again.

Love,

Amy

Jo put the letters aside and went to spend some time with her other younger sister. Beth's health had been getting worse again. Jo could see how pale and thin her sister was becoming.

'Jo, I know that I'm dying,' said Beth one evening. 'That is why I was so sad to see my sisters leaving last year. I did not know if I would see you all again.'

Jo didn't want to believe it, but the more time they spent together the more she knew that it was true. Mr and Mrs March had feared it for some time, and a great sadness filled their days together.

Chapter Eleven

Laurie met up with Amy in the south of France during his trip away with Mr Laurence. Amy studied Laurie's face as he filled her in on the news of his travels with his grandpa. She suddenly felt shy. Laurie had changed. He was no longer a boy, but had grown into a handsome young man.

'Beth has been very sick. Mother has told me in her letters,' said Amy. 'I feel I should go home, but they have told me not to cut my trip short as I'll never get this chance again.'

Laurie moved closer to her. 'I think they're right. After all, you are due to return in a couple of months. You'll be home before you know it. You being here and happy will bring them comfort, my dear,' said Laurie.

Amy liked Laurie calling her 'my dear'. They spent the afternoon strolling along the river and enjoying each other's company.

It was soon time for them to go back to the hotel. Amy was delighted to find out Laurie was attending the same party as she was that evening.

When she was dressed and ready, she went to wait for Laurie downstairs in the reception of the hotel.

Laurie didn't speak when he first saw her. She looked beautiful. The pair went to the party together. While Amy agreed to dance with a couple of others, Laurie had secured most of the dances with her. It was clear that there was something new blossoming between them.

Back at home, things were gradually getting worse for Beth. The March family put their grief to one side and tried to make Beth's last weeks as enjoyable as possible. They moved her into the brightest room of the house and gathered everything she cherished the most around her: flowers, her dolls, her cats, Amy's drawings, her father's books, Jo's desk and her mother's comfy chair all found their way into the room. Meg came round often with the children. They never failed to make Beth smile.

'How beautiful this all is,' said Beth, admiring the bright room, her possessions and the company of her family. But her delighted glow soon began to fade. She became so weak that even her sewing needle was too heavy for her to pick up.

Jo fell asleep on the sofa one evening. Beth wanted Jo to read to her but she wouldn't wake her older sister. Beth was grateful for all of the things Jo had been doing for her, and her sister deserved a rest. Beth decided to read to herself. She picked up Jo's book and a piece of paper fell out of it. Inside was a poem Jo had written about Beth. It brought Beth to tears.

The next morning Beth greeted her sister with a warm embrace. 'Oh Jo, do I really mean this much to you?' She held out the poem.

'That and so much more,' said Jo, laying down next to her.

'Then I don't feel as though my short life has been wasted. It's a comfort to know that someone loves me so much.'

'I can't bear the thought of losing you,' whispered Jo, as tears streamed down her face.

'I am not scared, Jo. Carry my love for you with you always.'

The day came when Beth took her last breath. The March family grieved together with tears and prayers.

The days after Beth's funeral were dark for Jo. She was heartbroken and lost. There was a large void in her heart where Beth had been.

Chapter Twelve

Dear Mother,

My heart aches. Although I will be home soon, I wish I was there now to comfort you all. I didn't get to say goodbye to Beth. I dream about telling her how much I love her every night.

But I have some happy news, too. Laurie has asked me to marry him, and I've said yes. I'm worried how Jo will take my news, though. She was always so much closer to Laurie when we were younger, and I'd hate for her to think I've stolen her best friend. Especially now Beth has gone.

I'm so happy, Mother. Our time together has brought Laurie and I so close.

Love,

Amy

Mrs March told Jo the news about Amy and Laurie. At first, Jo was silent.

'Are you happy about the news, Mother?' she asked.

'I am. I had hoped this would happen when Amy wrote to tell us she had been spending time with Laurie. But how do you feel about it, dear? I know how lonely you have been since we lost Beth.'

'I feel sad for myself,' said Jo. 'But I am glad Amy loves Laurie. She will look after him and he will look after her.'

Mrs March smiled at the wise, kind woman her daughter had become.

Amy and Laurie didn't tell anyone when they were returning home. Laurie crept into the March house and found Jo lying on the sofa with her eyes closed. She stirred at the noise.

'Oh my! Laurie! You're home!'

She sat up and threw her arms around him.

'You're glad to see me then?' he laughed.

'Of course I am,' Jo squealed. 'Where's Amy?'

'My wife is at Meg's house,' Laurie grinned. 'They'll be here soon.'

'Your what?' Jo paused as she realised what this must mean. 'You got married already? Why didn't you tell us?'

'We wanted it to be a surprise.' Laurie filled Jo in on the events of the past few months. After a while, Amy arrived with Meg and her family. The Marches were together again and it was the happiest Jo had felt since Beth had passed away.

'This calls for a celebration,' cried Mr March.

Hannah disappeared into the kitchen to prepare food and drinks. The family gathered around the table in the warmth of each other's company. Jo admired the sight of her family all together, but she still felt lonely.

Jo's thoughts turned to Professor Bhaer in New York. She had missed him since she had been home, and realised in that moment just how much she cared for him. She may have even fallen in love with him.

'Come and dance with me!' called Amy. Jo shook the thought of the professor out of her head and joined in the celebrations.

After a day of dancing, happiness and food, there came a knock at the door. When Jo went to answer it, she found Professor Bhaer standing there, smiling brightly at her. He was in town on business and had looked her up to visit.

'Oh, I'm so glad to see you!' cried Jo.

'And I you! But you are having a party. I'll come back another time.'

'No you won't. Please come in,' said Jo, guiding her friend into her home.

Professor Bhaer was given a warm welcome by the March family; they all liked him instantly. As they

talked to him throughout the evening, everyone found him to be kind and clever. More importantly, they noticed how he made Jo smile.

The professor became a frequent visitor at the March household. Jo spent a lot of time with him, and he helped her get through her grief after losing Beth. One day, as the two were walking together, Professor Bhaer stopped and took Jo's hands.

'Jo, I have nothing to offer you but my love. Do you have room in your heart for me?'

Jo could spend hours talking to Professor Bhaer about everything and anything. What's more, he had always been supportive of her writing. Jo knew that her family was what made her happiest, and Professor Bhaer already felt like a part of her family. 'Yes!' she said.

Epilogue

The March sisters had grown into fine women. They held their sister Beth in their heart always. Amy and Laurie had a daughter who they named Beth in her memory. The couple decided that they would use their wealth to help people in need.

Meg and John's twins, Daisy and Demi, grew up to be clever and adoring children. Jo married Professor Bhaer, much to the delight of her family.

Shortly after Jo's wedding, Aunt March passed away and left Jo her mansion in her will. Jo decided to turn the mansion into a school for rich and poor children alike. With Professor Bhaer at her side, Jo cared for the children and gave them the best education they could wish for.

After a while, Jo and Mr Bhaer had two of their own sons too. Soon Jo's home was full of happy children, running free. A part of Jo still wished to write another novel, in time. But with a life full of love, she was the happiest she had ever been.

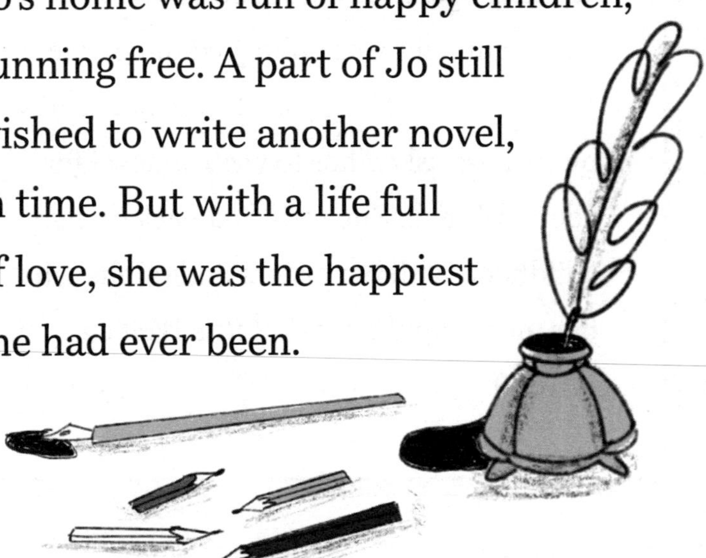

Louisa May Alcott

Louisa May Alcott was born in Philadelphia in 1832. Her father believed all children should enjoy learning, which inspired Alcott to read and write from an early age. In 1854, Alcott's first poem Sunlight was published under the pseudonym A.M. Barnard. One of Alcott's publishers asked her to write a novel for young women. She reflected back on her childhood with her sisters and published her most popular work, *Little Women*, in 1860.